THE LIFE OF JACK SPRAT
HIS WIFE & HIS CAT

PAUL GALDONE DREW THEM

McGraw Hill Book Company NEW YORK • TORONTO • LONDON • SYDNEY

To Allie and Don

Jack Sprat could eat no fat,
His wife could eat no lean,
And so between them both,
They lick'd the platter clean;

Jack ate all the lean,
Joan ate all the fat,
The bone they pick'd it clean,
Then gave it to the cat

When Jack Sprat was young,
  He dressed very smart,
He courted Joan Cole,
  And he gained her heart;

In his fine leather doublet,
  And old greasy hat,
O what a smart fellow
  Was little Jack Sprat.

Jack Sprat was the bridegroom,
  Joan Cole was the bride;
Jack said, from the church
  His Joan home should ride;

But no coach could take her,
The lane was so narrow,
Said Jack, then I'll take her
Home in a wheelbarrow.

Jack Sprat was wheeling
His wife by a ditch,
The barrow turn'd over,
And in she did pitch;

Says Jack, she'll be drown'd,
But Joan did reply,
I don't think I shall,
For the ditch is quite dry.

Jack brought home his Joan,
　　And she sat on a chair,
When in came his cat,
　　That had got but one ear;

Says Joan, I'm come home puss,
　　Pray how do you do,
The cat wagg'd her tail,
　　And said nothing but mew.

Jack Sprat to live pretty
    Now bought him a pig,
It was not very little,
    It was not very big,

It was not very lean,
    It was not very fat,
It will serve for a grunter,
    For little Jack Sprat.

Then Joan went to market
To buy her some fowls,
She bought a jackdaw
And a couple of owls;

Jack Sprat bought a cow,
His Joan for to please,
For Joan she could make
Both butter and cheese,

Or pancakes, or puddings,
    Without any fat.
A notable housewife
    Was little Joan Sprat.

Joan Sprat went to brewing
  A barrel of ale,
She put in some hops
  That it might not turn stale,

But as for the malt,
  She forgot to put that.
This is sober liquor,
  Says little Jack Sprat.

Jack Sprat went to market,
And bought him a mare,
She was lame of three legs,
And as blind as a–bat,

Her ribs they were bare,
For the mare had no fat,
She looks like a racer,
Says little Jack Sprat.

Jack and Joan went abroad,
    Puss took care of the house,
She caught a large rat
    And a very small mouse,

She caught a small mouse
And a very large rat.
You're an excellent hunter,
Says little Jack Sprat.

Now I have told you the story
Of little Jack Sprat,
Of Little Joan Cole,
And the one-ear'd cat.

Now Jack has got rich
  And has plenty of pelf,
If you'd know any more,
  You may tell it yourself.

PAUL GALDONE *gathered background material for this and other forthcoming books on a recent trip to England. The 900-year-old church sketched in the book is near Oxford, where he stayed. Mr. Galdone lives and works in Rockland County, New York.*